# THE CLASS FROM THE
# BLACK LAGOON

STORY BY
## MIKE THALER

PICTURES BY
## JARED LEE

Cartwheel
·B·O·O·K·S·®

## SCHOLASTIC INC.
New York   Toronto   London   Auckland   Sydney
Mexico City   New Delhi   Hong Kong   Buenos Aires

**To kids in every grade, you are all very special—M.T.**
**To my wife P.J., who's in a class all by herself—J.L.**

**visit us at www.abdopublishing.com**

Reinforced library bound edition published in 2014 by Spotlight, a division of the ABDO Group, PO Box 398166, Minneapolis, MN 55439. Spotlight produces high-quality reinforced library bound editions for schools and libraries. Published by agreement with Scholastic, Inc.

Printed in the United States of America, North Mankato, Minnesota.
102013
012014

 This book contains at least 10% recycled materials.

### Library of Congress Cataloging-in-Publication Data

This title was previously cataloged with the following information:

Thaler, Mike, 1936-
  The class from the Black Lagoon / by Mike Thaler ; pictures by Jared Lee
  p. cm. -- (Black Lagoon)
  Summary: On the first day of a new school year Mrs. Green's imagination runs wild as she thinks of all the horrible things she's heard about her new class, including that they've sent their previous three teachers into early retirement.
  1. Fear--Fiction. 2. Schools--Fiction. 3. Teachers--Fiction. 4. First day of school--Fiction. I. Title. II Series.
PZ7.T3 Ckf 2002
[Fic]--dc23                                    2003268235

ISBN 978-1-61479-194-2 (Reinforced Library Bound Edition)

All Spotlight books are reinforced library binding
and manufactured in the United States of America.

It's the first day of school, and I have a new class coming in one hour. I heard they're *really* weird and that they put their last three teachers into early retirement.

I also heard that when the class gets to school, they all turn into horrible ghouls! And they emit odd odors and make strange sounds.

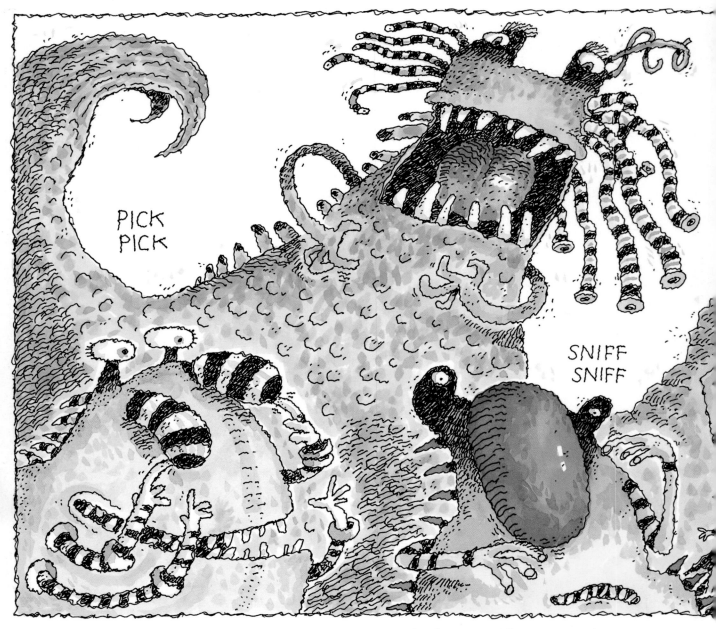

Some grow two noses so they can pick them at the same time.
They love *scratch* and *sniff*.

I heard that some have orange hair, some have green hair, some have purple hair, and some have *no hair*!

They're great at making horrible faces. They can roll their eyeballs
back into their heads so only the whites are showing.

And some can cover both their noses with their lips and wiggle their ears.

They can wrap their bodies in and around their chairs so tightly that sometimes they have to be pried off with crowbars.

One teacher said they tie themselves to their desks with their shoelaces.
I guess it's a safety precaution.

I heard they eat crayons, chalk, and erasers. They drink ink, chew pencils, love to mumble, and tear paper into tiny little bits.

They also make spitballs the size of cannonballs.
But the thing they're best at making...is noise!

They're all virtuosos with Velcro,
and drummers with pencils.

Every part of their bodies is a musical instrument.
Put it all together and you have a symphony orchestra.

Their other area of expertise is *excuses*.

"We were late because the school bus was attacked by pirates."

And they're *always* late when they come to school.
But they only come when they have highly contagious diseases.

When they're *healthy*,
they stay home.

In class, they're always waving their hands in the air
to go to the bathroom or to give silly answers like,
"What's George Washington's last name?"
"Bridge!"

They do love to write. They write on their desks, they write on the walls, and they write on each other. The only thing they don't write on...is their papers.

Instead of dotting their *i*'s and crossing their *t*'s, they cross their *eyes* and dot their *teeth*.

There are other things about school they love:
pestering teachers, poking peers, and using the
electric pencil sharpener. They call it Mr. Shred.

And he runs all day because they break their points on purpose
just to use him, over and over and over again. At the end of the day,
I'll be standing waist-deep in pencil shavings.

Oh, my, it's almost 8 o'clock! I'd better check
my survival kit: helmet, hockey pads, earplugs.
Well, I guess I'm ready.

Wow! They're all cheery and clean,
and each one has only one nose.

"Here's an apple and some flowers, Mrs. Green."
"Well, thank you, class."

The flowers were picked from the front of the school,
and the apple had sixteen bites out of it. But, hey,
no one's perfect. It's the thought that counts.

I'm going to love this class.